WHERE THE BLUEBELLS LIE

Linda Denise Smith

ISBN: 979-8-9947147-0-6
First Edition: 2026
Printed in the United States of America

DEDICATION

This book is dedicated to the memory of my parents,
who taught me to believe in dreams.
To my loving husband, my partner, my best friend,
and my constant support, whom I love always.
And to my sisters and brothers,
who pushed one another to rise higher.
My love to you all.

CONTENTS

ACKNOWLEDGEMENTS

Writing this book was a dream come true, filled with sleepless nights, long hours, and moments of doubt, but it became a milestone

I was able to achieve. And I did not do it alone.

To my loving husband, thank you for listening as I read each chapter again and again, for sitting beside me over countless cups of coffee, and for never growing tired of hearing my words. Your patience, love, and encouragement carried me through. I love you with all my heart.

To my editor, Annie T., I owe special gratitude for transforming my manuscript into a polished and professional work. Your skill, insight, and dedication are remarkable, and I am forever grateful.

To my sisters and brothers, thank you for your unwavering encouragement throughout this journey. Your love and support mean more than I can say.

And finally, to the readers who choose to take a chance on my debut story, thank you. This book now belongs to you as much as it belongs to me.

Chapter 1

The House with the Long Drive

The morning sun pierced the humid mist, casting light over the long driveway of the antebellum house. Hailey Winston stepped out of the car and paused, her eyes drawn to the tall windows lining the front of the home. She had never pictured herself living somewhere like this, an old historic house in Greensville, Virginia.

Moving had never been easy for her. As a military child, she had grown used to packing up her life every few years, leaving schools and friendships behind before they had time to settle. Stability had always felt temporary, something other people had.

Now, standing here with Ethan by her side, married and finally putting down roots, she wondered if this house was different. Maybe this time, stability wasn't just a fleeting idea, it could be real. Or maybe she was still chasing the idea of it.

Ethan parked beside her and leaned casually against the car, wrapping his arms around her waist.

"Mrs. Winston," he teased, "why are you standing out here when you should be inside?"

Hailey chuckled softly, still staring at the house.

"It never occurred to me that I'd end up living in a place called Greensville."

Ethan laughed. "Is that a good thing or a bad thing, Mrs. FBI?"

"You mean former FBI," she said, smiling.

"Will you miss it?" he asked, nodding toward the life they had left behind in Washington, D.C.

Hailey shook her head slowly. "I doubt I'll miss the traffic. Or the long walks between government buildings. Or Union Station at rush hour."

Ethan grinned. "I'll miss parts of it. But I missed Virginia more. That's why I came back. That's why I ran for district attorney."

Hailey fell quiet. His words settled between them, heavier than she expected. She looked back at the house, at the tall windows watching them from the front of the property.

Footsteps on gravel broke the moment.

An elderly woman walked up the long, winding driveway, moving at an unhurried pace.

"Hello there," she said warmly. "I'm Helen Hickman. I just wanted to welcome you to the neighborhood."

"Thank you," Ethan replied. "I'm Ethan Winston, and this is my wife, Hailey."

Helen's face brightened. "Oh, I recognized you. I voted for you."

"I appreciate that," Ethan said with a polite smile.

"When I heard you were moving in, I was thrilled," Helen continued. "This house has always been my favorite.

Those windows… they're just beautiful."

Ethan nodded. "Thank you. We're glad to be here."

Hailey returned the smile, but something about Helen's tone made her chest tighten. She couldn't explain it, and that bothered her.

"My son, Michael, moved in with me a few years ago after my husband passed," Helen added. "I live right across the street."

"I'm sorry for your loss," Hailey said softly.

"Thank you. Moving can be exhausting, so I won't keep you," Helen said, already stepping back. "We work hard to keep this neighborhood special."

The words lingered longer than they should have.

Hailey watched as Helen turned and walked back down the long, twisting driveway. She didn't look back. Her figure slowly disappeared behind the hedges and trees, swallowed by the property across the way.

We work hard to keep it that way.

The phrase echoed in Hailey's mind, stripped of its polite tone. She crossed her arms as a faint chill slid through her despite the warm morning air.

A moving truck rumbled up the driveway, snapping her out of it. Three men jumped down and began unloading boxes.

Ethan headed toward them, already speaking with the movers.

Hailey stayed where she was, her eyes drifting once more toward the hedges where Helen had vanished.

For reasons she couldn't yet name, the house suddenly felt less like a beginning and more like something waiting.

Chapter 2

Watching from a Distance

Morning light spilled through the tall window as Hailey sipped her coffee. A year had passed since she and Ethan moved to Greensville, Virginia. Leaving her job as an FBI agent behind had not been easy, but her new role at the Greensville Daily Post was beginning to feel like the right decision. Some mornings, like this one, she even believed the move had been worth it.

Ethan rushed down the stairs, already buttoning his jacket.

"I'm going to have to skip breakfast," he said. "I will grab something at the office."

Hailey smiled faintly. "Coffee and a donut?"

"You know me too well," Ethan said, leaning in to kiss her cheek.

"Why are you rushing to work so early?" she asked.

"I'm meeting with my team before I see Chief O'Connor."

"Must be a big case."

"It is." He glanced at his watch. "What about you?"

"I'll be at the office around ten. There's a flea market I've been meaning to check out first. It's not far."

Ethan nodded. "I'll call you later."

Hailey watched from the window as he drove away.

A short while later, she grabbed her bag and headed out.

The flea market was already busy when she arrived. Voices overlapped, music drifted from somewhere in the distance, and the smell of old wood and dust hung in the air. Hailey wandered through the aisles, unhurried, until a glint of brass caught her eye.

The antique clock sat on a narrow table, its surface worn but carefully maintained. The craftsmanship was unmistakable. Hailey leaned in, her eyes tracing every detail. She didn't hesitate long before deciding to buy it.

As the vendor rang her up, Hailey felt it, a subtle shift in awareness she had learned to trust. She looked up.

An older Black woman stood across the aisle, watching her. Not browsing. Not distracted. Just watching. When their eyes met, Hailey offered a polite smile and a small nod. The woman returned it, calm and unreadable.

Beside her stood a middle-aged Black man, holding what looked like a folded quilt against his chest. He said nothing.

Hailey's unease wasn't fear. It was recognition, the sense of being noticed for a reason she didn't yet understand. She finished the purchase quickly, thanked the vendor, and moved on.

She got into her car and started to pull away from the flea market. She glanced in the rearview mirror.

The elderly Black woman was still watching.

Hailey drove on, her grip tightening slightly on the steering wheel.

That was strange, she thought. Not threatening. Just… strange. And it stayed with her longer than it should have.

Later that morning, Hailey sat at her desk at the Daily Post, sunlight slanting through the blinds. Her fingers hovered over the keyboard, but she wasn't typing. Her thoughts kept circling back to the flea market, and to the woman's steady gaze.

A knock at her office door pulled her back.

"Come in."

Becca Lockhart stepped inside and closed the door behind her. She didn't sit. Her eyes swept the room once, then settled on Hailey.

"Hi," Becca said. Her tone was casual, but her body was tense.

"What's going on?" Hailey asked.

Becca hesitated. "Can I ask you something off the record?"

Hailey studied her. "That depends."

"How long did you work for the government?"

"Long enough," Hailey said. "Why?"

"Because I found a case. It was closed years ago. It shouldn't have been."

Hailey felt the familiar pull, sharp and unwelcome.

"What case was that?"

"Not here," Becca said quietly. "I don't trust this building as much as people think I should."

That made Hailey pause.

"You came to me for a reason," Hailey said.

Becca met her eyes. "Because you don't belong here yet. And because you know how to see what people try to hide."

She turned to leave, then stopped.

"And Hailey?" Becca said softly. "If you start looking into this… don't let anyone know you're looking."

Then she left.

Hailey stared at the closed door, the image of the woman at the flea market flashing through her mind. For the first time since moving to Greensville, she felt certain of one thing: she wasn't just being welcomed. She was being watched.

As Hailey gathered her notes to leave for the day, her young secretary stepped quietly into the office.

"Mrs. Winston," she said, holding out a sealed envelope. "Someone dropped this off for you earlier. He didn't give a name."

Hailey took the envelope. It was unmarked. No return address. No stamp. She opened it slowly, her fingers careful, almost reluctant.

Inside lay a single sheet of paper.

The message was handwritten.

"If you want answers, come alone. Cedar Creek Park. By the fountain. This evening."

Hailey folded the note once and slipped it into her purse. The uneasy feeling she'd had all day settled deeper in her chest. Someone had been watching her.

Chapter 3

A Mother's Plea

It was late evening, though the sun still hung high in the sky. Hailey pulled into Cedar Creek Park and parked near the fountain. Two people waited nearby, an elderly Black woman seated on a bench and a middle-aged Black man standing just behind her.

She remembered them from the flea market. The strange elderly woman and the man who had been watching her.

Hailey took a deep breath, heart racing, and approached them. The woman stood as she drew near.

"My name is Annabelle Colts," she said, extending her hand. "Please, call me Anna."

Hailey shook her hand. The grip was firm and warm.

She kept her left hand tucked in her pocket.

"It's nice to meet you, Anna."

"This is my son, Damin," Anna said.

Damin nodded, his expression guarded.

Hailey sat beside Anna. "I'm Hailey Winston."

"I know who you are," Anna said quickly.

Hailey looked at her. "You do?"

"I followed your career in Washington," Anna said.

"You solved the Silent Killer case. I read your books, Criminality, Parts One and Two."

Hailey shifted slightly. Praise made her uncomfortable. "Thank you."

Silence settled between them.

Damin shifted his weight and looked away.

Anna took a breath. "My daughter disappeared."

Hailey nodded slowly. "What was her name?"

Anna swallowed. "Liana. Liana Colts."

The name settled between them.

"She was five years old," Anna continued. "It's been thirty years."

Hailey exhaled. "Before you go any further, I need to be clear, I'm no longer with the FBI."

"I know," Anna said. "That's not why I asked you here."

"The police stopped looking," Damin said quietly.

"A long time ago."

Hailey looked back at Anna. "And the FBI?"

"They tried," Anna said. "But after a while, everything went quiet. Files closed. Leads dried up." She hesitated. "They said it wasn't just Liana. There were four Black girls. All five years old. All taken on the same day."

Hailey felt the air shift around her.

"How?" she asked.

"They disappeared from school," Anna said. "Their parents came to pick them up, and the girls were nowhere to be found. Gone. Same day. Same hour."

A chill moved through Hailey.

She stood slowly. "I can't promise anything."

Anna looked up at her. "I'm not asking for promises."

Hailey nodded once. "I'll look into it. Quietly. But you can't talk to anyone else."

Anna stood and hugged her without warning. "Thank you."

"Get home safely," Hailey said.

Later, sitting alone in her car, Hailey stared through the windshield as the park lights flickered on one by one. The name kept repeating in her thoughts.

Liana.

Thirty years was a long time to wait for answers.

She started the engine of her car, knowing this was no longer just a story. It was someone's child.

Chapter 4

Midnight in the Archives

Hailey sat at the dinner table, barely touching her food. Her thoughts kept circling back to Anna and to the girls.

"How was your day?" Ethan asked, lifting his wine glass.

Hailey hesitated. "It was… unusual."

Ethan studied her for a moment, then nodded. "Mine was strange too. Something about Chief O'Connor. I can't explain it. It just didn't sit right."

Hailey nodded, letting him talk, though her mind stayed fixed on a name she couldn't shake.

Liana.

Dinner ended quietly. Later, they went to bed. Ethan slept beside Hailey, his breathing steady. She stared at the ceiling, waiting for sleep that refused to come.

She slipped out of bed and went to the library.

The microfilm reader hummed softly as the reel turned. A bright white beam cut through the dark room. She flipped through archived newspaper pages, date after date, year after year.

Then she saw it.

Four Black girls. Five years old. Disappeared from school. Same day. Same hour.

Liana Colts.

Her pulse quickened as she continued winding the reel. The case had gone cold thirty years ago. Closed quietly. Forgotten.

A creak sounded upstairs.

Hailey stood instantly and switched off the reader.

Light spilled down the staircase.

Ethan appeared in the doorway. "Hailey… what are you doing up?"

She turned, forcing calm into her voice. "I couldn't sleep."

He stepped closer and wrapped his arms around her.

"Everything okay?"

She nodded against his chest. "Yeah. Just one of those nights."

He kissed the top of her head. "Come back to bed."

She followed him, but her mind stayed behind in the dark library.

Before dawn, Hailey woke again.

She crossed the hall to the library. The microfilm reader was still warm from earlier, its faint hum filling the quiet room. She fed another reel into place and began flipping through archived newspapers and public records.

The more she read, the less sense it made. Dates shifted. Names appeared once, then vanished. Reports contradicted each other.

Someone had edited the past.

The phone in the kitchen rang.

Ethan looked up from the table.

Hearing it from the library, Hailey hurried down the hall and lifted the receiver before the second ring finished.

"Hello?"

"It's Becca," came the voice on the other end. "Can we meet? Somewhere quiet."

Hailey paused. "What's this about?"

"I've been looking into the missing girls," Becca said softly. "Off the record. You need to see what I found, but not at the office."

Hailey glanced toward the window. Shadows stretched across the street, long and still.

"Go on," Hailey said.

She tightened her grip on the receiver, her reflection faint in the dark glass.

This wasn't curiosity anymore. It was responsibility.

Chapter 5

The Upper Room

Barlow Creek Café sat just off the main highway, easy to miss if you weren't looking for it. Hailey slid into the booth across from Becca, noticing how Becca kept glancing toward the front windows.

"How do you know about the case?" Hailey asked quietly. "The four missing Black girls?"

Becca wrapped her hands around her coffee cup. "It started two years ago. I met a man named Henry Winley. Everyone called him O'Henry. He owned a honey store outside of town."

Hailey listened.

"He used to bring me jars of honey," Becca continued. "We became friends. I'd stop by his store sometimes on my way to work. About six months ago, I went out there and found he'd been moved to a county home. Alzheimer's. His mind was slipping, and he wasn't doing well. He couldn't remember things clearly, and simple tasks became impossible for him."

Becca swallowed. "When I visited him, his thoughts drifted in and out. But no matter what, he kept saying the same thing, over and over."

"What thing?" Hailey asked.

"'I saw those Black girls.'"

Hailey stiffened.

"He'd mutter about the school. About the woods," Becca continued. "Sometimes he'd say, 'They know.' Other times, he'd say nothing at all."

Becca exhaled slowly. "I started digging. The case didn't add up. Files missing. Timelines off. Everyone said the girls vanished from school, but there were gaps everywhere."

"And O'Henry?" Hailey asked.

"Before he died, he kept repeating something. Over and over." Becca lowered her voice. "'In the box. On the bed.'"

Hailey felt a chill.

"Two days later, I went back to his store. I searched the house. Nothing. Just old photos." Becca reached into her bag and slid a few pictures across the table.

Hailey studied them: O'Henry, a woman, and a young boy.

"I don't know who they are," Becca said. "But something didn't feel finished. So I went back yesterday."

She paused.

"There's an upper room in the back of the house,"

Becca said. "Dust everywhere. Old furniture. It felt… wrong being in there." Her voice lowered. "There was a small bed pushed against the wall. I began to search that area. I moved the bed away from the wall and noticed a rug. I lifted it. The floorboard underneath was uneven, slightly off in color, and loose."

She swallowed.

"I lifted the board. That's where the box was."

Hailey didn't speak.

"I took it," Becca said. "And I left before someone saw me."

Hailey held her breath.

Becca reached into her bag again and pulled out the box.

Inside were yellowed newspaper clippings. And a small sock.

A child's sock.

Hailey stared, her chest tightening. "This means he knew," she said quietly.

Becca nodded. "Or he saw something. I don't know which is worse."

Hailey leaned back, thinking fast. "We can't handle this alone."

"Who can we trust?" Becca asked.

"I have a friend," Hailey said. "Marcus Lambert.

Private investigator. He owes me a favor."

Becca nodded. "What do you want me to do?"

"Keep digging," Hailey said. "Quietly. No one else."

"I will."

They stood. Hailey stayed seated a moment longer after Becca left, staring at the box.

This wasn't just a cold case. It was evidence.

And it meant someone had kept a secret for thirty years.

Chapter 6

Calling in a Favor

Hailey stood at the pay phone near the café entrance, gripping the receiver before dialing. It rang twicc.

"Hello?" a voice answered.

"Hi, is this Marcus?" Hailey asked.

"Yes, it is," he said. "I'd know that voice anywhere.

If it isn't Hailey Winston."

She smiled. "How the hell are you?"

"Good," Marcus replied. "How are you?"

"Marcus, I need your help."

There was a pause on the line. "You don't usually start a call like that."

"I'm looking into a case," Hailey said. "It's thirty years old."

Marcus exhaled. "You're not with the Bureau anymore. You're a journalist now. Why are you digging into a cold case?"

"I'll explain later," Hailey said. "Right now, I need your experience. I need you."

Silence stretched across the line.

"Alright," Marcus said finally. "Tell me what you know."

"Four Black girls went missing thirty years ago. All were five years old. The case went cold."

Marcus didn't respond right away. "What do you need from me?"

"Do what you do best."

Another pause. "I can be there in a day or two. I'm in Washington. Wednesday afternoon, if that works."

"It does," Hailey said.

"Give me the name."

Hailey hesitated only a moment. "Liana Colts. I met her mother yesterday," she added.

Marcus sighed. "I'll start looking into the case tonight. But, Hailey, be careful. This feels like a road you shouldn't walk alone."

"I will," she said.

Before he hung up, Marcus added, "Have you told Ethan?"

Hailey hesitated. "No."

"He's the district attorney," Marcus said. "If this turns dangerous, he needs to know."

"I know," Hailey said quietly. "I just don't know how to tell him yet."

"I'll call you when I land," Marcus said.

The line went dead.

Hailey lowered the receiver and stood still for a moment as people moved past the café entrance.

Telling Ethan wouldn't be easy. She already knew he wouldn't like this, especially not a case buried for thirty years.

She dropped another coin into the slot and dialed again.

"Hello?" Anna answered.

"Hi, Anna. It's Hailey Winston."

"Oh, hello," Anna said.

"I need to speak with you," Hailey said. "Could I come by this evening? Around five?"

"Yes," Anna said immediately. "That's fine."

"I'll see you then."

Hailey hung up and stepped away from the booth.

There was no turning back now.

Chapter 7

The Photograph

The evening air had cooled, and Hailey pulled on a light coat before stepping out of her car. Anna's house sat quietly at the end of the street, its porch light already on. For some reason, Hailey hesitated before walking up the steps.

She rang the doorbell.

"Mrs. Winston," Anna called. "Please, come in." "Please, call me Hailey," she said as she stepped inside.

Anna gestured toward the living room. "Have a seat."

Hailey nodded. She kept her coat and gloves on, despite the warmth of the house. Something about being there made her feel exposed.

Anna sat across from her. "Have you learned anything?"

Hailey didn't answer right away. Instead, she asked, "Can you tell me what Liana was wearing the day she disappeared?"

Anna's face softened. "Her favorite blue dress. She loved that dress. If I'd let her, she would've worn it every day." A faint smile crossed her lips. "I always tied a blue-and-white ribbon in her hair to match."

Anna's smile faded.

"She wore white socks," Anna added quietly. "Thick ones. Too thick for her shoes, but she refused to wear anything else."

Hailey felt something tighten in her chest.

"Did you ever meet the other mothers?" Hailey asked.

Anna shook her head. "No. That's what always

bothered me. No one could ever tell me who the other girls were. The papers just said "four Black girls." Only Liana's name ever appeared."

Hailey swallowed.

Anna stood. "I think I have a picture."

She disappeared down the hallway.

The room felt warmer now. Hailey slipped off her gloves and loosened her coat, resting her hands in her lap.

Anna returned holding a photograph.

Hailey reached out to take it.

Anna hesitated for only a second, then placed the photo in Hailey's hands.

For a moment, neither of them spoke.

"Here," Anna said quietly.

Hailey stared at the picture.

Liana stood, smiling in her blue dress, white socks pulled up to her calves.

The same kind of socks.

Hailey's breath caught.

She slid her gloves back on slowly. "May I keep this?"

Anna nodded, still watching her. "Yes."

Hailey stood. "Thank you."

She left without another word.

Outside, the air felt sharp against her skin. Hailey got into her car and closed the door, her heart pounding.

Something had shifted.

She didn't know what it meant yet, but she knew it couldn't be undone.

Chapter 8

A Place Called O'Henry's

ailey wasn't ready to go home. She drove past her house once, then again, before finally pulling into a small lot near the corner market. She sat with her hands on the steering wheel longer than necessary before shutting off the engine.

Anna's silence echoed in her mind, not what she had said, but what she hadn't. For the first time since the investigation began, Hailey felt certain her questions had stirred something that no longer wanted to stay buried.

She picked up the photograph again. This time, her eyes drifted past Liana's face to the background. Something about it felt wrong. Familiar, but out of place.

Hailey folded the photo and stepped out of the car.

The phone booth stood near the edge of the lot. She slipped inside, closed the door, and dropped a coin into the slot. The line clicked as she dialed.

It rang once.

"Hello?" Anna answered.

"Hi, Anna. It's Hailey," she said. "I was looking at the photo, and I noticed the background. I don't recognize it."

There was a pause on the line.

Anna's breathing changed. "It was taken at O'Henry's Honey Store," she said quickly.

Hailey didn't respond.

Anna continued, her words coming faster. "Liana loved that place. She always asked for the honey lollipops. That day, she insisted on coming with me. She wore her blue dress."

Anna stopped.

"O'Henry took the photo," she said more quietly. "He gave it to us that Christmas."

Through the phone, Hailey heard a voice in the background, Damin calling for his mother.

"Anna?" Hailey said.

"I have to go," Anna said quickly.

"Wait…"

The line went dead.

Hailey hung up and returned to her car. She sat there for a long moment, the engine still off. The street was quiet. She glanced toward the end of the block, then started the car and headed home.

The tires crunched softly as she pulled into her long driveway. She stayed in the car a second longer than necessary.

Chapter 9

The Name That Vanished

The next morning, Ethan hurried down the stairs, already dressed for work. "Honey," he said, "you were up late again. I saw the light on."

Hailey hesitated. It bothered her to hide things from him. They had always been honest with each other.

"Yes," she said. "I was."

Ethan leaned down and kissed her. "I've got an early meeting today. Don't worry about breakfast. I'll eat at the office. I'll call you later."

Hailey watched him leave, knowing the truth wouldn't stay buried much longer.

The kitchen phone rang.

Hailey lifted the receiver. "Hello?"

"It's Marcus," the voice said. "I got into Virginia late last night."

Her pulse quickened. "You found something?"

"I did," he said. "Something odd. But I need to check it before I say anything."

"What did you find?" Hailey asked.

"Not yet," Marcus said. "I'll call you later."

The line went dead.

Hailey stood for a moment, the receiver still in her hand. Whatever Marcus had seen, it had changed his tone.

She glanced at the clock and grabbed her keys. She was supposed to meet Becca at Marshall Elementary at ten.

Hailey and Becca arrived within minutes of each other. They exchanged a look before walking inside.

At the front desk, a woman with round glasses pushed low on her nose looked up. "Can I help you?"

"We're looking for archived attendance records,"

Hailey said. "From a long time ago."

"That information is confidential," the woman replied.

"I know," Hailey said quietly. She reached into her purse and briefly showed an old FBI identification card.

The woman glanced at it, then nodded. "Anything that old is archived. If you have a date, the records are on microfilm." She gestured toward a desk against the wall. "The reader's over there. I'll be in the office if you need me."

She walked away.

Hailey waited until the door closed.

Becca lowered her voice. "Okay."

Hailey sat at the microfilm reader and threaded the reel.

April 13, 1941.

The machine hummed softly as the reel turned. A projected image filled the glass viewing screen, faded ink, uneven handwriting, and names lined in careful rows. Beneath the header, a line read: Teacher, Zellee Freeman.

They searched slowly.

"There," Becca whispered.

Liana Colts.

Next to her name was a short note written in faint ink:

Not in school.

Hailey felt her chest tighten.

"Check the days before," Becca said.

Hailey wound the reel back. Liana's name appeared again, marked like the others. Normal. Routine.

"Now after," Becca said.

Hailey advanced the reel forward.

The next frame came into view.

Liana's name was gone.

Hailey blinked and wound forward again.

Nothing.

She checked the following frames. And the ones after that.

The class roster continued, but Liana Colts never appeared again.

There was no note beside her name.

No explanation.

Hailey checked the rest of the list, then another class, then another.

Every other child remained accounted for.

Only one name disappeared.

Hailey leaned back slowly, the weight of it settling in.

"There weren't four girls," Becca said quietly.

Hailey stared at the empty space where a child's name should have been.

"No," she said. "There was only Liana."

The room felt smaller than it had a moment ago, as if something old had been disturbed and didn't want to be found.

Chapter 10

The Visit

After leaving the school building, Hailey stood beside Becca's car.

"We need to talk with Ms. Freeman," Hailey said.

"I agree," Becca replied.

Becca had already looked up the number in the school directory. Hailey walked to the pay phone just outside the main entrance and dropped a coin into the slot. She dialed.

It rang twice.

"Hello?"

"May I speak with Ms. Freeman?" Hailey asked.

"This is Ms. Freeman."

"My name is Hailey Winston. I'm a journalist with the Greensville Daily Post. I have a few questions. May I come by today?"

There was a pause on the other end of the line.

"I think that will be fine," Ms. Freeman said finally. "How about noon?"

"That would be great," Hailey said. "I'll bring my colleague, Becca Lockhart."

Ms. Freeman gave the address, and Hailey thanked her before hanging up.

"I'll meet you there," Becca said.

Hailey nodded. "I need to stop by the office first.

There are some clippings I want to bring."

***

Becca was already there when Hailey pulled up to Ms. Freeman's house. They got out of their cars at the same time.

Hailey walked up to the door and knocked twice.

Ms. Freeman opened it slowly. Her hands trembled slightly as she gripped the doorframe.

"Ms. Freeman," Hailey said gently. "I'm Hailey, and this is Becca."

"Please, come in," Ms. Freeman said. "Have a seat."

They followed her into the living room.

"I just made coffee," Ms. Freeman said. "Would you like some?"

"No, thank you," Hailey and Becca said together.

Ms. Freeman sat across from them. "So… how can I help you?"

Hailey took a breath. "Ms. Freeman, do you remember a student named Liana Colts?"

Ms. Freeman's face changed instantly. Her mouth opened, then closed.

"Yes," she said softly. "Little Liana. She was so bright. She loved school. Did you know she could read at five years old? Such a joyful child."

Hailey reached into her bag and pulled out the photograph.

Ms. Freeman leaned forward. "That dress," she said. "She loved that dress. She always told me it was her favorite."

Hailey nodded. "According to these newspaper clippings…" she placed them on the table, "…Liana went missing from school on April 13th. They also say three other

Black girls disappeared that same day."

Ms. Freeman stood up suddenly.

"No," she said. "No."

Her voice shook. "That's not what happened."

She looked at Hailey sharply. "You don't ask questions like a journalist."

Hailey glanced at Becca, then back at Ms. Freeman.

"I used to work for the FBI," Hailey said quietly.

"But that's not why I'm here."

Ms. Freeman turned away, pacing.

"I told them," she said. "I told the police. I told the principal."

She stopped and faced Hailey again.

"Liana was not in school that day," Ms. Freeman said. "There were no other girls missing. Just Liana."

Her hands clenched.

"They told me to stop talking," she said. "They said

I was mistaken, that it happened anyway."

Hailey stepped closer. "Who told you that?"

Ms. Freeman swallowed. "The sheriff."

She hesitated, then spoke again, her voice dropping.

"He threatened me. He said if I don't stop talking, my house would burn. He said my husband would be ruined. He said I would be destroyed."

The room fell silent.

Ms. Freeman stared at Hailey's face. Then her eyes.

"And you," she said slowly. "Your eyes…"

She shook her head, as if pushing something away.

"They fixed the records," Ms. Freeman continued.

"Made it look like she was in school."

She pressed a hand to her chest.

"I kept the originals. I made sure they showed the truth before I stopped teaching."

Her voice softened, tired now.

"It haunted me. Every day. I was so afraid. Everyone was. The sheriff was powerful. He had friends."

She stopped speaking.

Hailey and Becca stood.

"Thank you, Ms. Freeman," Hailey said. "If you remember anything else, please call me. And please, don't talk to anyone else."

Ms. Freeman nodded silently.

Outside, Becca leaned against her car. "What is happening?" she asked.

Hailey shook her head. "It's bigger than I imagined."

"I'll meet you at the office," Becca said.

Hailey nodded and drove back to the Daily Post.

She had just set her purse on her desk when her young secretary appeared at the doorway.

"Mrs. Winston," she said, "you have a call on line nine. Mr. Marcus Lambert."

Hailey's stomach tightened. She picked up the receiver.

"Hello?"

"This is Marcus," he said. "I need to meet with you right away."

Hailey didn't hesitate. "There's a place called Barlow Creek Café, right off the main highway."

"On my way," Marcus replied.

She hung up slowly, her grip tightening on the receiver.

Chapter 11

A Case Meant to Die

Hailey sat in a booth at the café, choosing a corner where they wouldn't be noticed. She lifted her coffee to her lips and looked up as Marcus walked through the door. She waved to him.

They hugged tightly.

"Good to see you again, Hailey," Marcus said.

"You too," Hailey replied.

Marcus slid into the booth across from her. He placed a folder on the table, thick with copies of files, police reports, and old newspaper clippings.

"Hailey," Marcus said quietly, "I did some digging into this case. I've never seen anything like it. No wonder it went cold. It was meant to."

Hailey leaned forward. "What do you mean?"

"The more I looked, the worse it got," Marcus said. "Conflicting times. Missing signatures. Reports that don't match each other. Details that should be there, but aren't."

He tapped the folder. "The case was confused on purpose."

"How were you able to get all this?" Hailey asked.

Marcus shrugged slightly. "You know how it is. You used to work at the Bureau. I still have friends. People who remember Greensville."

Hailey nodded. "Go on."

"What bothers me most," Marcus continued, "is that the investigation never truly focused on whether it was four girls or one. It didn't focus on finding Liana at all."

He paused.

"Instead, everything points back to the same names: Sheriff John Lee Recker, his inner circle, and O'Henry."

Hailey frowned. "But O'Henry is dead."

"I know," Marcus said. "But he was never brought forward as a witness. The FBI never took this case. In the 1940s, with segregation and the war, no one was going to push hard for a missing Black child."

Hailey sat back, unsettled.

Marcus lowered his voice. "Here's the part you need to hear carefully. I found out where Sheriff Recker is now. He's alive. Living in a county home about two hours from here."

Hailey stiffened. "You're going to talk to him."

"Yes," Marcus said. "Tomorrow morning."

"I need to be there," Hailey said immediately.

Marcus shook his head. "No. Not yet. Trust me. I have a plan."

Hailey's jaw tightened. "Marcus…"

"I'll call you after," he said firmly. "We'll meet again."

Reluctantly, Hailey nodded. "Okay."

They stood and left the café together. As Hailey walked to her car, one question pressed against her chest harder than all the others.

Where is Liana?

She put the car in drive and headed home.

Chapter 12

Room 212

Marcus arrived at the county home and paused near the front desk before approaching a nurse.

"Excuse me," he said. "I'm looking for a resident named John Lee Recker."

The nurse glanced at her list. "Room 212. You can take the stairs around the corner to your left."

"Thank you," Marcus said.

Room 212 was at the end of the hall. The door stood open. Marcus knocked lightly.

"Come in," a tired voice called.

John Lee Recker lay in bed with the television on low. The flickering screen cast light across his face, as if the TV were watching him instead.

"Are you John Lee Recker?" Marcus asked.

"Yes," the old man said.

"My name is Marcus Lambert. How are you today?"

Mr. Recker squinted. "I'm doing fine. Why are you here?"

"I've been reviewing some old files," Marcus said.

"I have a few questions about a case from the 1940s. You were the sheriff of Greensville County, correct?"

Mr. Recker's mouth curved into a grin. "I was sheriff a long time," he said. "I controlled the town."

Marcus let that sit.

"On April 13, 1941," Marcus continued, "records show four Black girls were taken from Marshall Elementary School. Were you the one who handled that investigation?"

Mr. Recker repeated the words slowly. "Black girls... Black girls..."

"Yes," he said finally. "I investigated. It was a long case. I never found the girls. The Negroes knew something."

Marcus kept his voice steady. "With respect, Mr. Recker, the records don't add up. There are no witness statements. No clear timelines. Do you remember interviewing anyone?"

Recker's eyes drifted. "It was handled," he muttered. "All under control."

"What about the girls?" Marcus pressed. "Was it really four, or just one?"

Mr. Recker went silent. His eyes fixed on the ceiling.

"I looked for the girls," he said slowly. "I looked for her."

Marcus straightened. "Her? Who is she?"

"The girls," Recker said, though his voice faltered.

Marcus turned toward the window. A framed photograph sat on the ledge. He picked it up and held it closer.

"That's a nice photo," Marcus said.

Mr. Recker took it, his hands trembling slightly.

"That's my wife, Lauren," he said quietly. "I miss her."

"And the boy?" Marcus asked.

Mr. Recker smiled faintly. "My son. My only son. John Jr."

"Your son?" Marcus repeated.

"Yes," Mr. Recker said. "Army boy. Always wanted to join. But he can't leave."

Marcus watched him closely.

Before he could ask another question, Mr. Recker's breathing deepened. His eyes closed. He had fallen asleep.

Marcus placed the photo back on the ledge and left the room.

Sitting in his car, Marcus stared straight ahead.

"He can't leave."

Marcus opened his folder and wrote one line across the top of a page: John Lee Recker Jr. — Army.

He closed the folder, slid it onto the passenger seat, and started the car.

Chapter 13

Behind the Uniform

Marcus had slept no more than four hours. Most of the night had been spent staring at notes spread across the small hotel desk, fitting pieces together that refused to sit neatly. The case felt less like a straight line now and more like a puzzle that had been deliberately broken.

Before dawn, Marcus used the hotel phone to contact a high-ranking military officer in Washington. He explained only what was necessary. The officer listened carefully, asked precise questions, and said little, but when the call ended, Marcus knew the door had opened.

By morning, arrangements had been made. A sealed envelope containing restricted military records would be waiting for Marcus when he arrived. No explanations. No commentary. Just the truth, documented and undeniable. Only then did Marcus book his flight.

As he gathered his things, the weight of it settled in. The case wasn't unraveling. It was resisting. Before leaving for the airport, Marcus called Hailey from the hotel phone.

"Hello?" she answered.

"Hailey, it's Marcus."

"Where are you?" she asked quickly. "I tried calling the hotel all day yesterday."

"I got the message," he said. "I'm heading to the airport. I'm flying to Kansas."

"Kansas?" Hailey repeated. "What's in Kansas?"

"Yes," Marcus said. "But I can't explain right now."

"Marcus, what did you find? Is this about Sheriff Recker?"

"Hailey," he said sharply.

She stopped.

"Do you trust me?" he asked.

"Yes," she said without hesitation.

"Then let me do my job," Marcus said. "Keep digging on your end. And Hailey, tell Ethan. He's the district attorney. He'll find out."

The line went dead.

Hailey lowered the receiver slowly.

Kansas. Military records. Whatever Marcus had uncovered, it had shifted something.

***

Early that afternoon, Marcus arrived in Kansas. An hour later, he stood inside the facility as a sealed envelope was placed into his hands without comment. Everything had already been arranged.

He waited as John Jr. was brought into the room.

The years had settled into the man's face, yet the resemblance to his father was unmistakable.

Marcus sat across from him.

"Mr. Recker," he said evenly. "My name is Marcus Lambert. I'm a private investigator."

John Jr. said nothing.

"I'm looking into a historical matter involving your father."

"My father?" John Jr. repeated.

Marcus opened the folder. "You enlisted young. Eighteen."

"So?" John Jr. said, a faint grin appearing and then disappearing.

"You lived in Greensville before you enlisted," Marcus continued. "You drove a pickup truck then."

John Jr.'s jaw tightened.

"What kind of truck was it?" Marcus asked. "And where did you spend most of your time?"

John Jr. leaned back. "I'm not answering that."

Marcus didn't move. "Your father was very protective of you."

John Jr.'s eyes flashed. "So what?"

"Your father always protected you," Marcus said quietly.

The chair scraped back.

"This interview is over," John Jr. said. He stood and walked out without looking back.

Marcus remained seated as the guard closed the door.

Something about the reaction didn't sit right. Not anger. Not fear.

Control. And control meant the truth was still being held.

Chapter 14

Hidden in Plain Sight

It was late when Marcus checked into a small hotel near the airport. His flight back east wouldn't leave until early afternoon, but sleep didn't come easily. The case had come undone in his hands, and nothing sat where it was supposed to anymore.

He spread the files across the table: records, reports, notes, and fragments of interviews Sheriff Recker claimed had been conducted decades ago. Marcus read them again, slower this time, searching for what had been missing.

His eyes returned to the interview Becca had done with O'Henry.

O'Henry liked taking photographs.

The thought stayed with him.

Marcus picked up the photograph Becca had found: Liana, standing in front of O'Henry's store. He studied her face, the set of her eyes, the way she stood. A chill settled in his chest.

He lifted a magnifying glass from the desk and leaned closer.

Through the store window, barely visible, sat a dark pickup truck. Old. The wheels looked unusual. And standing near it was a young male. Seventeen, maybe eighteen. Too old to be a child. Too young to feel harmless.

Marcus lowered the glass.

The image of another photograph surfaced in his mind, the one he'd seen in Sheriff Recker's room. A woman. A child. A son.

The pieces didn't fit.

He poured a drink but didn't raise it. His eyes drifted to the large sealed envelope resting on the table. Marcus set the glass down, untouched.

He opened the envelope.

The documents inside made him stand.

"No," he whispered. "That can't be."

He stared at the pages, his breath shallow, the room suddenly too quiet.

The truth hadn't just survived. It had been hidden.

$$\mathcal{C}hapter\ 15$$

The Sealed Envelope

Marcus woke early the next morning, steadier than he had felt in days. Sleep had done what thinking could not. He gathered the documents spread across the table, arranged them carefully, sealing everything before slipping the envelope into his briefcase.

Using the hotel phone, Marcus called the airport. He canceled his flight to Virginia and booked another, this time to Washington. As he hung up, he stood at the window for a moment, wondering what he would find once he arrived.

He glanced at the clock. It was time to call Hailey.

The phone rang twice before she answered.

"Good morning, Hailey," Marcus said.

"Morning, Marcus. Are you in Virginia?"

"No," he said. "That's why I'm calling. I booked a flight to Washington. I need to follow a lead."

"A lead?" Hailey asked. "Can you tell me more?" "Not right now," Marcus said. "I spoke with someone connected to military records. I need time to confirm something before explaining."

There was a pause.

"I'll be leaving around ten," Marcus continued. "I should be back in Virginia later this evening. I'll call you then."

"Okay," Hailey said. "Have a good flight. Please call as soon as you can."

"I will," Marcus said. "Talk soon."

They hung up.

Marcus arrived in Washington late that afternoon and drove to the Fairlawn Historic Community, a quiet neighborhood of large homes and long-settled families. He parked in front of a stately house set back from the street, its age and careful upkeep immediately apparent.

He rang the doorbell.

"Yes?" a voice called.

"Marcus Lambert," he said when the door opened.

"I'm Earl Williams," the man said. "Please come in. You can have a seat in the study."

Marcus thanked him and explained that he was a private investigator following up on historical military relocation records. The conversation unfolded slowly, cordial, careful, occasionally uneasy. Despite his age, the man's memory was sharp. He offered coffee and coffee cake and shared more than Marcus had expected.

Marcus's eyes drifted toward a framed photograph on the shelf beside the window. He picked it up gently.

"That's a nice photo," Marcus said. "Is this your wife?"

Mr. Williams nodded. "Yes. That's her." He paused.

"She passed about seven years ago."

Marcus glanced back at the photograph. "And the girl?"

"That's my daughter," Mr. Williams said. "She's about ten in that picture."

Marcus studied the image a moment longer, husband, wife, child standing close together, then placed the frame back exactly where it had been.

"I'm sorry for your loss," Marcus said.

"Thank you," Mr. Williams replied.

They moved on, and the conversation shifted back to records and dates. Still, the image stayed with Marcus long after. They spoke for over an hour.

As Marcus drove away, a familiar tightening settled in his chest. Something had shifted. He hadn't found answers, but he had disturbed something that had been carefully kept still.

That evening, back at the hotel, Marcus placed the sealed envelope on the table and stared at it for a long moment. He poured himself a beer but barely touched it.

Tomorrow, he would return to Virginia.

Tomorrow, he would decide what to say.

$Chapter\ 16$

No More Secrets

Hailey rose early that morning. Sleep had been slipping away from her more often than usual. She stood in the kitchen with a cup of coffee, staring out the window, her mind already turning over the case before the day had even begun.

The phone rang.

She crossed the room and lifted the receiver before the second ring finished.

"Hello?" Hailey said.

"Morning, Hailey," Marcus said.

She straightened. "Marcus, are you back?"

"Not yet," he said. "My flight leaves this afternoon.

I just wanted to touch base."

"Okay, but…"

"I'll call you when I land," Marcus interrupted gently. "We'll talk then. But Hailey… you need to tell Ethan what's going on."

There was a pause.

"I will," she said.

"I'll see you later this evening." "Okay. See you soon."

Hailey placed the receiver back on the hook slowly, Marcus's words settling heavily in her chest.

Marcus hung up, then paused. He had planned to call Hailey when he landed, but he knew he needed to see Ethan first.

***

Footsteps sounded on the stairs.

"Hey, honey," Ethan said as he entered the kitchen.

"Who was that?"

"Marcus," Hailey said, still distracted.

"How's the old guy doing?" Ethan asked, pouring himself coffee.

"He's… he's doing well," she said, then caught herself. "Sorry. Yes, he's fine."

She hesitated, then said quietly, "Do you want breakfast?" She was already reaching for the pan.

Ethan didn't answer right away. He watched her for a moment.

"Hailey," he said, "I'm worried about you. You're not sleeping. You're up most nights. Your mind's somewhere else."

She stopped what she was doing. "I know. And I'm sorry."

She turned to face him. "I owe you the truth."

Ethan didn't interrupt.

"I took on a thirty-year-old case," she said. "I didn't plan for it to happen, but it pulled me back into investigation.

I didn't know how you'd react."

"Which case?" Ethan asked.

"The missing Black girls," Hailey said. "From the school."

He nodded slowly. "I know."

She froze. "You know?"

"I'm the district attorney," Ethan said calmly. "Files don't just disappear on their own. And I know you. The late nights. The way you go quiet when something matters."

She swallowed. "I should have told you."

"Yes," he said gently. "You should have."

Then he stepped closer. "But I understand why you didn't."

Relief washed over her.

"I'm sorry," she said again.

Ethan pulled her into his arms. "We'll deal with it together."

They stood there quietly, looking out the window as the morning light filled the kitchen.

For the first time in days, Hailey felt like she could breathe.

Chapter 17

Tracing the Steps

It was a cool afternoon when Marcus drove to Ethan's office. Molly, his secretary, looked up as he approached.

"May I help you?"

"Yes," Marcus said. "My name is Marcus Lambert.

I'm here to see Mr. Winston."

She nodded. "He's expecting you. Just a moment."

She dialed the extension. "Mr. Winston, Marcus Lambert is here."

"Send him in," Ethan said.

Marcus stepped into the office. The two men shook hands.

"How are you, Marcus?" Ethan asked.

"I'm doing well," Marcus replied, taking the seat across from his desk.

Marcus glanced around. "Nice office."

Ethan smiled. "Thank you. But I don't think you came all this way to admire the furniture."

They both laughed lightly.

"I know Hailey told you we've been investigating the case of the four missing Black girls," Marcus said.

"She did," Ethan replied. "And the more I look at it, the stranger it becomes. The case was tucked away and forgotten."

Ethan stood and walked to an oval table, motioning Marcus over. Files were already spread out.

"I had everything pulled from unsolved crimes this morning," Ethan said. "Timelines, reports, statements."

Marcus leaned over the documents. "The timeline doesn't make sense," he said. "The locations don't match."

"I agree," Ethan said. "And there's something else. I was about seven years old when the girl went missing. My parents talked about it constantly."

Marcus looked up. "Did they ever mention names?"

"Only one," Ethan said. "Liana. No one ever talked about the others."

"That's what bothered me," Marcus said. "It feels like the story was widened to blur the truth."

Ethan nodded slowly. "Exactly." He straightened. "Let's go."

Marcus looked at him. "Where?"

"We're going to walk the path," Ethan said. "The one no one ever questioned."

They drove past Anna's house and parked partway down the road. Both men stepped out and looked at the distance.

"She would have walked this," Ethan said.

They followed the route until they reached O'Henry's Honey Store.

Marcus pulled out a photograph. "Look at this," he said. "You can see the reflection in the window. That black truck was parked about fifty feet from the store."

Ethan studied it. "Her brother said Liana walked slowly," he said. "She liked to look around."

Marcus nodded. "She disappeared on April 13th." Ethan froze.

"In April," Ethan said slowly, "there's a trail here.

We called it the Bluebell Trail. It blooms every spring, with light blue flowers stretching through the field. It's right across from O'Henry's store."

Marcus looked at him. "That would draw a child."

Ethan's face tightened. "She wouldn't have gone straight to school."

Marcus folded the photo. "We need to get back to your office."

"Why?" Ethan asked.

"I remember something," Marcus said. "Something I need to show you."

They turned back toward the car, urgency settling between them as Ethan started the engine.

Chapter 18

The Mark on the Shoes

Hailey sat at her desk, leaning back in her chair, twirling an ink pen between her fingers. She stared out the window, lost in thought.

A knock came at the door.

"Come in," Hailey said.

Becca stepped inside.

"Any new leads?" Hailey asked.

"Not yet," Becca said.

Hailey stood and began pacing the room. "We're missing something."

"We already established it was one girl, not four," Becca said. "We went through the records."

"That's true," Hailey said. She stopped suddenly. "But the missing piece is here. I can feel it."

She moved to the table where photographs and documents were spread out. Becca joined her.

Hailey grabbed a blank sheet of paper and began writing.

"When I investigate a case," she said, "I start with the who, what, where, when, and why."

"We know the when," Becca said.

Becca focused on the records, while Hailey studied the photographs. For a long moment, neither spoke.

Then Hailey leaned closer.

"Is it strange to you," she said slowly, "that in every photo, Liana is wearing the same blue-and-white dress? The same socks. The same shoes?"

Becca nodded. "Her mother said she loved that dress. She wore it every chance she got."

Hailey gave a small smile, then her expression shifted.

"But the shoes," Hailey said quietly. "Why were they never clean?"

She picked up one photo, then another. "Look at the laces. One string is short. The other is long. Every time."

Becca leaned in. "It's the same in all of them." "And here," Hailey said, pointing. "Do you see it? A faded mark. It looks like an 'L.'"

She traced the mark lightly. "She marked her shoes.
For Liana."

Becca exhaled. "O'Henry took so many pictures."

They exchanged a look, both thinking the same thing.

They spread more photographs across the table.

Hailey stopped.

"Becca," she said. "Look at this."

It was a photograph taken in front of O'Henry's store. A little white girl stood near the entrance, smiling. A woman stood beside her.

Becca stared. "Oh my God."

"The shoes," Hailey said. "They're the same."

Silence filled the room.

"Who is that woman?" Becca asked.

Hailey shook her head slowly. "I don't know." She looked at the photograph again, her pulse quickening. "But I think it's time Marcus and Ethan saw this."

Chapter 19

The Girl in the Photograph

Hailey and Becca arrived at Ethan's office. "Hi, Mrs. Winston," Molly said from the front desk. "You can go right in. Mr. Winston is expecting you."

Hailey and Becca entered the office. Ethan stood and briefly kissed Hailey on the cheek. Files were already spread across the large table. Marcus arrived moments later, slightly out of breath from hurrying in. They all sat down.

"I think we've got a lead," Ethan said.

Marcus and Ethan shared what they had found. Ethan explained how they decided to walk the path Liana would have taken.

"Liana never made it to school. In April, the Bluebell Trail blooms across from O'Henry's store, a field full of blue flowers. Enough to pull a child off the road."

Hailey leaned forward. "Remember, her mother said she loved blue and white. That trail could have caught her attention."

"Exactly," Ethan said. "I think she stopped following her brother and wandered toward the trail."

"Now we have a timeline," Becca said.

"But there's more," Marcus added. "I walked the path farther out. There's a black shed set back from the trail. Whoever owned that shed would've seen something."

"Not necessarily," Hailey said.

Marcus turned toward her. "What do you mean?"

Hailey spread several photographs across the table.

"Look closely, first the socks, then the shoes, then the laces." They leaned in.

"In every photo," Hailey said, "the laces don't match.

One side is always longer."

"And there," Marcus said quietly. "That faint mark. An 'L.'"

Ethan studied the photos carefully. "Remarkable." "O'Henry took a lot of pictures," Becca said. "And here's another one."

Hailey slid a photograph forward.

Marcus stared. His mouth fell open. "That little girl is wearing Liana's shoes."

Ethan picked up the photo. "Then who is she?"

"If we find out who she is or the woman standing beside her, they may have seen who took Liana," Becca said. "They never found a body. No trail. Nothing."

Ethan looked at Marcus. "Do you think Liana could be alive?"

Marcus didn't answer.

There was a knock at the door.

"Come in," Ethan said.

"I'm sorry to interrupt," Molly said, stepping inside.

"I need your signature on these forms."

She handed Ethan the papers. As he signed, Molly glanced down at the photographs on the table. She paused.

"Lilly was so young back then," Molly said softly. "She must have been about six."

The room went still.

Marcus stared at the little girl in the picture, his jaw tightening. "Then who is she?"

"Molly," Ethan said slowly, "do you know this girl?"

"Yes," Molly said. "That's her mother, Ms. Pickett. She passed away years ago."

"How do you know Lilly?" Marcus asked.

"We went to school together," Molly said. "Before my parents moved to Upper Virginia. I was about ten when we moved."

"Do you know where she lived?" Marcus asked.

"Plainview, Virginia," Molly said.

Ethan handed her the signed forms. "Thank you, Molly."

Molly nodded and left.

Becca stood. "I'm heading to the county office. I'll pull the public records on Lilly Pickett."

"Call me as soon as you find anything," Hailey said.

"I'll talk to Molly again," Becca added. "See if she remembers more."

Becca left.

Marcus looked at Hailey and Ethan. "I think we just cracked it."

Chapter 20

The Hidden Shed

Becca returned from the county office and confirmed that Lilly Pickett was still living in Plainview, Virginia, the daughter of Susan Pickett.

Hailey reached out, and Lilly agreed to meet the following day. Hailey told Ethan and Marcus that she and Becca would speak with her, and they agreed.

The next morning, Hailey and Becca drove two hours to Plainview. Hailey parked beside a modest house and shut off the engine. She knocked, and a woman opened the door.

"Are you Lilly?" Hailey asked.

"Yes."

"I'm Hailey Winston. This is Becca."

Lilly stepped aside. "You can come in. Have a seat in the front room."

Hailey sat forward. "I'm a journalist. I'm looking into an old case from about thirty years ago. Do you remember the story about four Black girls missing from Greensville?"

Lilly nodded slowly. "I was little back then. But I remember it."

"Can you tell us what you remember?" Becca asked.

Lilly picked up a soda from the table and took a long drink before speaking.

"I remember a Black girl running. She was screaming."

Hailey's chest tightened. "Where were you?" she asked.

"In a shed," Lilly said. "My brother used to take me there so he could smoke without my mom knowing. He always brought me along as an excuse. I liked the honey."

"What happened when you heard the screaming?" Hailey asked.

Lilly hesitated. "My brother closed the shed door and locked it. But there was a small hole. We could see through it." She paused. "I saw a blanket around her."

"Did you see who took her?" Hailey asked.

Lilly shook her head. "No. It was too far away."

"Why didn't you tell anyone?" Becca asked.

Lilly's voice dropped. "My brother made me swear. He said if I ever told anyone, he'd hurt me. He said they'd come after our family."

"So, you never told anyone," Hailey said softly.

Lilly nodded.

"Where is your brother now?" Hailey asked.

"Michael died in a car accident five years ago."

Hailey pulled out a photograph. "Do you recognize this?"

Lilly's face changed. "That's the picture O'Henry took."

Hailey lifted another photo. "Can you tell me about the shoes you're wearing here?"

Lilly frowned. "I don't remember getting them. My mom gave them to me."

"Do you know where she got them?" Hailey asked. Lilly shook her head. "No."

Hailey took a breath. "Do you remember if the little girl had shoes on?"

Lilly hesitated. "I... I don't remember."

Becca leaned in. "You mentioned honey in the shed.

What did you mean?"

"O'Henry stored honey there sometimes," Lilly said. "Honey lollipops, too. It was his shed. He didn't know my brother went in there."

Lilly folded her hands. "I'm sorry. That's all I remember."

"That's fine," Hailey said. "Thank you for talking with us."

***

Back in the car, neither of them spoke.

Finally, Becca said, "She saw more than she's saying."

Hailey nodded. Lilly had seen who took Liana and had carried that truth for thirty years.

Hailey started the engine and drove back toward Greensville.

Chapter 21

Too Close to Ignore

Hailey called Marcus late that evening. She told him about Plainview. About Lilly Pickett. About the shed behind O'Henry's store, the honey, the screaming, the shoes.

Marcus listened without interrupting. He didn't take notes. He didn't ask questions. Some details didn't need recording. They settled into place on their own.

When Hailey finished, there was a pause on the line.

"Marcus," Hailey said. She repeated his name.

"I'm listening," he replied.

"You don't sound excited about what I found," Hailey said carefully.

"That's not it," Marcus said. "I'm processing what you told me."

"Where do we go from here?" Hailey asked.

Marcus hesitated. "Let's talk tomorrow," he said. "Get some rest."

"All right," Hailey said. "Good night."

They ended the call.

Marcus remained seated at the small table, the lamp still on. The envelope lay open in front of him, its contents spread neatly but untouched. He already knew what the records said. He had known the moment he first saw them.

Over twenty years of investigating cases like this, Marcus had learned when the truth was close and when it was dangerous. This case hadn't stalled because the evidence was weak. It had stalled because no one wanted to touch it.

He thought about the photographs again. The details others had overlooked. The way the pieces fit too cleanly once placed side by side.

Marcus closed his eyes and took a slow breath. Then he opened them and looked at the documents again, as if repetition might change what he had already seen.

It didn't.

He glanced at the clock and reached for the phone. Tomorrow morning, he would meet with Ethan. They needed to compare notes, timelines, records, and facts. Confirmation mattered.

Especially now.

Marcus turned off the lamp and went to bed, knowing the case wasn't finished.

But it was close. Too close to ignore.

Chapter 22

The Truth Redirected

Marcus arrived at Ethan's office just before ten, carrying four large envelopes tucked under his arm. He knocked once on the door.

"Come in," Ethan said.

Marcus stepped inside. "Morning."

"Morning," Ethan replied, glancing up from his desk.

He nodded toward the table. "Give me a minute."

Marcus set the envelopes down and remained standing while Ethan finished signing paperwork. His attention was already on the files spread out across the table.

"How's Hailey?" Marcus asked.

"She left early," Ethan said. "Didn't say where she was going."

A moment later, Ethan joined him at the table. Reports, timelines, and witness statements, everything tied to the case, lay open on the table.

Marcus spoke first. "This case never involved four Black girls."

Ethan nodded. "No. It didn't."

"One girl," Marcus continued. "Liana Colts."

"And she wasn't taken from school," Ethan said.

"The records don't support that," Marcus replied. "Attendance logs. Teacher statements. The timing doesn't line up."

Ethan leaned back slightly. "Which means the investigation was directed away from the truth."

"Yes," Marcus said. "If she wasn't taken from school, then the school became the cover."

Ethan looked over the files. "Four girls sounded bigger. More confusing. Easier to lose."

Marcus placed a map on the table. Two locations were circled in pencil: the school and O'Henry's store.

"I walked the path farther than the reports ever did," Marcus said. "The shed across the road from O'Henry's store sat directly in the line of sight. Whoever handled the investigation intended to mislead."

Ethan studied the map. "She liked blue."

"Enough to wander," Marcus said.

They sat in silence.

"The truth didn't disappear," Marcus added. "It was redirected."

Ethan nodded once. "Which means we've been looking where we were told to look."

Marcus closed the folder. "And not where it actually happened."

Neither of them spoke after that.

They didn't need to.

Chapter 23

The Missing Piece

It was afternoon when Marcus called Hailey from his hotel.

"Hello," Hailey said.

"Hi, Hailey. It's Marcus."

"Hi," she replied. "Is everything okay?"

"Hailey, I need to talk with you. Alone. Today."

She didn't hesitate. "Is it the case?"

"Yes," Marcus said.

Ethan wouldn't be home until late that evening. She knew that immediately.

"That'll be fine," she said. "I was planning to leave the office early anyway. Meet me at the house around four."

"That works," Marcus replied. "I'll see you then."

They hung up.

Marcus arrived at Hailey's house a little before four.

He sat in the car for a moment before putting it in park, steadying himself. He checked his briefcase, ensuring the files were in order, then walked up to the door.

Hailey opened the door. "Come in, Marcus."

She led him into the kitchen. They sat across from each other at the table. For a moment, neither spoke.

"Hailey," Marcus said finally, "what I'm about to tell you, I need you not to interrupt. Not yet."

She nodded. "Okay."

"This case took a turn I never expected," Marcus said. "I dug deeper than I planned to. And once I did, the pieces stopped fitting the way they were supposed to."

He opened his briefcase and laid several documents on the table.

"I need you to look at these," he said. "Carefully."

Hailey picked up the first record. A birth document.

Her eyes scanned the page, then stopped.

A defect documented at birth.

Marcus slid another paper toward her. "This is a military relocation record," he said. "No dependents listed."

Then another. "And this appears later. A child added. No birth certificate. Same defect."

Hailey read without speaking. Her breathing slowed. She moved the papers closer, lining them up, reading again as if the words might rearrange themselves.

They didn't.

She leaned back slightly and looked down at her left hand.

Her pinky was smaller and underdeveloped, something she had lived with her entire life without questioning.

The room suddenly felt too quiet.

She looked up at Marcus.

"Am I… Liana?" she asked.

Marcus didn't answer immediately. He didn't soften it.

"The records indicate that you are," he said.

Hailey stared at him, stunned. The words didn't arrive all at once. They settled slowly, heavily.

She pushed her chair back from the table and stood.

Marcus remained seated.

Neither of them spoke.

Chapter 24

Nothing Was an Accident

The evening had grown late, and Marcus had long since gone. Hailey stood alone in the living room, staring out through the tall picture window of the antebellum house. The glass reflected her back at herself, but she barely recognized the woman staring back.

She heard Ethan's car pull into the long driveway. Gravel crunched beneath the tires. The sound felt distant, as if it belonged to another life.

Ethan entered through the kitchen door.

"Hailey?" he called.

When she didn't answer right away, he poured himself a glass of wine.

"Hailey?"

"I'm in the living room," she said.

He stepped in and stopped short. One look at her told him something was wrong.

"Are you alright?" he asked carefully. "What's going on?"

She turned to face him. "Honey, I need to talk to you."

Ethan set the glass down and sat on the couch, resting his hands on his knees. Hailey sat beside him but didn't look at him yet. She waited until the house was quiet, until there were no footsteps, no passing cars, no distractions.

"Ethan," she said softly, "Marcus confirmed something in the records. And it points to me."

Ethan didn't speak. His jaw tightened, then relaxed.

He stayed still.

"He came by this afternoon," Hailey continued. "He needed to speak with me alone. What he found wasn't speculation. It wasn't theory. It was there, on paper."

She swallowed.

"The records don't place me where I was supposed to be."

Ethan looked at her now.

"My parents never had children," she said. "There's no birth record. No hospital documentation. Just… silence. And then later, a child appears in the records. Without explanation."

She took a breath. "That child has a documented birth defect."

Ethan frowned slightly.

Hailey slowly placed her left hand over his. She didn't speak. She didn't need to.

Ethan's eyes dropped to her hand. To her pinky.

He froze.

When he looked back up at her, his eyes were wet.

"Nothing about you was an accident," he said.

"Hailey," he said quietly.

She nodded once. A single tear slid down her cheek.

"I didn't remember," she said. "I still don't. But the records don't lie."

Ethan pulled her into his arms, holding her tightly, as if afraid she might disappear if he let go.

"You're not alone," he said. "Not now. Not ever."

Hailey closed her eyes, leaning into him.

For the first time since the truth began closing in around her, she let herself breathe.

Chapter 25

Mother and Daughter

It was a cool Saturday morning. Bright early sunlight filled the room, waking Hailey. She had already been up for a while, sitting on the edge of the bed, watching the light stretch across the floor. She stood and glanced at Ethan, still sleeping. Quietly, she moved toward the door, hoping the creaking stairs wouldn't wake him.

She went to the kitchen, her favorite room, and made coffee. Sitting at the table, she spoke softly to herself, as if saying the words aloud might make them easier to face.

"I must talk to Anna. How can I tell her? What can I say?"

She sipped her coffee, feeling tears welling up.

Ethan came down the stairs. "Good morning, honey. How are you feeling?"

Hailey gave him a faint smile.

Ethan poured himself a cup of coffee and sat across from her. Hailey looked at him. "I must talk to Anna today. I have to."

"Call her," Ethan said gently.

Hailey walked across the kitchen and slowly lifted the phone. She dialed. It rang once before Anna answered.

"Hello," Anna said, her voice soft.

"Hi, Anna. This is Hailey," she said, her voice trembling. "How are you?"

"I'm doing fine, Hailey."

"I need to speak with you. May I come by this afternoon? Around two?"

"Of course," Anna said. "I'll see you then."

They hung up.

Ethan looked at Hailey. "It's going to be alright."

That afternoon, Ethan drove Hailey to Anna's house.

He parked in front. As he moved to get out of the car, Hailey placed her gloved hand over his.

"No," she said softly. "I must go in alone."

Ethan nodded. "I'll be right here if you need me."

Hailey walked to the front porch, took a deep breath, and knocked gently twice.

Anna opened the door. The house was silent.

Anna looked into Hailey's eyes, then down at her left hand.

Without being asked, Hailey slowly removed her glove.

Anna reached out and touched Hailey's hand. Tears filled her eyes.

Hailey stepped forward, and they embraced.

"How long have you known?" Hailey whispered.

"The first time you came here," Anna said through tears. "When you grew warm and removed your glove… I saw your hand. I knew."

"Did you ever stop searching for me?" Hailey whispered.

"Never," Anna said. "Not for a single day. I searched. I prayed. I begged God not to let me die with a broken heart."

Anna held Hailey's face in her hands, her thumbs trembling against her cheeks.

"I am your mother," she whispered.

Then, as if saying it aloud made it real at last, she added softly, "Liana."

Chapter 26

Where the Bluebells Lie

The next day, Ethan and Hailey landed in Washington in the late afternoon. Ethan rented a car and drove toward Fairlawn. As they entered the neighborhood, Hailey remembered it exactly as before, quiet, respectable, ordinary. A place that had once been home, without her ever knowing why.

They arrived at Earl Williams' house. The same house Marcus had visited. Ethan parked in the driveway and gently held Hailey's hand.

"It'll be alright," he said.

Hailey gave a faint smile.

Ethan stepped out and opened her door. Together they walked to the front porch. Hailey knocked twice.

The door opened.

"Hailey," Earl said gently. He kissed her cheek. "Hi, Ethan," he added, giving him a brief hug.

They settled in the living room. Silence hung heavy between them.

"Dad," Hailey said finally, "I need to talk to you. I have questions."

Earl's face tightened. "I knew this day would come," he said quietly.

"I believe you found me when I was a child," Hailey said.

Earl nodded. There was no point denying it.

He looked straight into her eyes.

"I was driving along a rural road. I saw a little girl lying near the edge of the woods. Barefoot. Silent. Terrified. I looked around, but no one was there. No cars. No adults. Nothing. I picked you up and took you home to my wife. She tried to comfort you. But you wouldn't speak."

He placed his hand over Hailey's.

"We wanted children, but we couldn't have any," he said. "We didn't know what else to do."

"Why didn't you look for my parents?" Hailey asked.

Earl exhaled slowly.

"We were afraid. And when the Army relocated us, it became easier to disappear. Your mother wanted to tell you many times, especially as you got older. But you were happy. And we were happy to have you."

"But I wasn't yours," Hailey whispered.

Tears filled Earl's eyes.

"I'm so sorry, Hailey."

He stood.

"I kept something. I'll be right back."

Earl returned from the attic carrying a small box. He placed it in Hailey's hands.

"Your mother and I couldn't throw it away. We knew one day you'd need the truth."

Hailey opened the box.

Inside lay a long-faded ribbon and a blue-and-white dress, dirt still clinging to the fabric. In the pocket, she found a crushed bluebell petal.

She lifted the dress carefully. Brought it close to her face. Breathed in, as if she could still smell the sweetness of honey, the bluebell fields, the warmth of a childhood she never remembered. She pressed the fabric gently to her cheek.

"I always loved this dress," she whispered. "It was my favorite."

She opened her eyes slowly.

"My name is Liana Colts," she said.

She turned to Ethan, tears streaming down her face.

"Ethan… I know who took me in the fields."

ABOUT THE AUTHOR

 Linda Denise Smith writes mystery and suspense fiction exploring women's strength, hidden histories, and small-town secrets. A graduate of the University of Michigan, she spent years teaching in public schools, an experience that deepened her love of storytelling and human connection.

Where the Bluebells Lie is her first published novelette and the fulfillment of a lifelong dream to bring imagined worlds and forgotten voices to life on the page.

She is a member of the Women's Fiction Writers Association (WFWA). When she is not writing, Linda enjoys reading mystery novels, quiet mornings with coffee, and spending holidays with family and friends.

www.ingramcontent.com/pod-product-compliance
Lightning Source LLC
Chambersburg PA
CBHW020604160726
47991CB00002B/863